Caillou
And The Big Slide

Adaptation of the animated series: Jeannine Beaulieu
Illustrations taken from the animated series and adapted by Eric Sévigny

COOKIE JAR

Caillou and his daddy were spending the afternoon at the playground. Caillou loved the swing, especially when Daddy pushed. "Higher, Daddy, higher!" Caillou shouted. From his swing, Caillou saw Clementine. Caillou loved playing with Clementine. Whenever they played on the train, she let him be the engineer.

"Let's go down the slide," Clementine suggested.
"Let's go down the big slide. It's much more fun."
Caillou and Clementine ran over to the big kids' area.
Caillou stopped in front of the slide and stared up in
surprise. It looked so high! Caillou was afraid to climb up.

Caillou looked around the playground and saw the play tunnels. The large, brightly colored tubes didn't look nearly as scary.

"Let's play in the tunnels first," Caillou suggested.

"Okay," said Clementine. "Try and catch me."

Daddy was sitting on a bench watching Caillou and
Clementine play.
"Caillou, we'll have to go home soon," Daddy said,
looking at his watch.

"Let's go down the slide," Clementine said.
"You first," Caillou said.
Clementine climbed up and pushed herself
off at the top and was at the bottom before
she had time to shout "whee"!
"That was fun!" she exclaimed. "Now it's your turn."
"Okay, okay," Caillou mumbled.

Caillou climbed up slowly, clinging to the handles and repeating, "I'm not scared. I'm not scared."
But when he reached the top, he was shaking with fear. Clementine looked very small to him, way down at the bottom of the slide. He could hardly hear her shouting, "Slide, Caillou! Slide!"

Caillou was terrified. He couldn't move.
"Daddy, Daddy!" he cried.
Clementine told Caillou's daddy, "I think Caillou's scared.
I wasn't scared a bit," she said.
"You're a big girl, Clementine. You can do lots of things."

Daddy climbed the ladder.
"Hmm, this slide is pretty high, isn't it?"
Caillou nodded.
"I know what we can do, Caillou. Let's go
down together. It'll be fun, you'll see."
Daddy held Caillou's hand.
"Are you ready, Caillou?"
"Ready, Daddy."

"One, two, three, here we go!"
Caillou was thrilled.
"Did you see that, Clementine?
I came down the big slide!"
"I came down all by myself,"
she told him.

"So can I," Caillou insisted. "I'm not scared anymore."
Caillou climbed back up and whizzed down the slide,
shouting, "Look at me-e-e-e!"
"Good for you, Caillou," Daddy said.
"I'm proud of you! You're a big boy."

"It's time to go home now."
"Just one more time, please, Daddy!"
Caillou ran back to the ladder with
Clementine close behind.
One, two, three, whee! And of course,
that wasn't the last "one more time"!

Adaptation of text by Jeannine Beaulieu based on the scenario of the CAILLOU animated film series
produced by Cookie Jar Entertainment Inc. (© 1997 CINAR Productions (2004) Inc.,
a subsidiary of Cookie Jar Entertainment Inc.).
All rights reserved.
Original story written by Christel Kleitch.
Illustrations taken from the television series CAILLOU and adapted by Eric Sévigny.
Art Direction: Monique Dupras

The PBS KIDS logo is a registered mark of PBS and is used with permission.

We acknowledge the financial support of the Government of Canada through
the Canada Book Fund for our publishing activities.

Canadian   Patrimoine
Heritage   canadien

We acknowledge the support of the Ministry of Culture and Communications
of Quebec and SODEC for the publication and promotion of this book.
SODEC
Québec

Bibliothèque et Archives nationales du Québec and Library and Archives
Canada cataloguing in publication

Beaulieu, Jeannine, 1934-
Caillou and the big slide
New ed.
(Clubhouse)
Translation of: Caillou et la grande glissade.
Originally issued in series: Backpack Collection. c2001.
For children aged 3 and up.

ISBN 978-2-89450-867-1

1. Fear - Juvenile literature. 2. Fathers and sons - Juvenile literature. I.
Sévigny, Éric. II. Title. III. Series: Clubhouse.

BF723.F4B4213 2012   j152.4'6   C2011-942121-6

Printed in China
10 9 8 7 6 5 4 3 2 1   CHO1819 JAN2012